WAY OF THE ODYSSEY SHORT STORY COLLECTION VOLUME 4

CONNOR WHITELEY

No part of this book may be reproduced in any form or by any electronic or mechanical means. Including information storage, and retrieval systems, without written permission from the author except for the use of brief quotations in a book review.

This book is NOT legal, professional, medical, financial or any type of official advice.

Any questions about the book, rights licensing, or to contact the author, please email connorwhiteley@connorwhiteley.net

Copyright © 2024 CONNOR WHITELEY

All rights reserved.

DEDICATION

Thank you to all my readers without you I couldn't do what I love.

A TRUTH AND A LIE

If you asked any of the tens upon tens of trillions of humans in the Imperium how they would get access to forbidden knowledge, then there were only ever three answers. The most probable would be, they would simply report you to the authorities and you would never ever be seen again. The second answer would be you shouldn't because that is simply immoral and an affront to humanity and the Truth that the Rex lies about.

The third answer would be to find some kind of abomination like an alien, a historian or some kind of other forbidden creature that possessed such knowledge. The only problem with such things was that they were rarer than rare and you would most probably die in the process.

Thankfully that was not a problem for Commander Jerico Nelson.

Thick aromas of alcohol, sweat and wonderfully sweet chocolate filled Jerico's senses as he went inside

The Lover's Bar onboard the disc-shaped space station known as Outpost-66.

Jerico smiled as he leant against the wonderfully warm grey metal doorway where a handful of people were coming and going. They were clearly military cadets judging by their cleanly pressed grey uniforms, and Jerico almost wanted to ask them where the hell they were off to.

It wasn't normal for any military units to be this far from civilisation, but he couldn't do that because he was hunted, keeping a low profile and he just couldn't draw attention to himself. And it wasn't like the military of the Imperium wasn't a massive Cult, if he spoke to the wrong person, then Earth would be told sooner or later.

Jerico shook his head at the very notion of Earth finding him.

Jerico hated how the entire bar was awful as a strategic position if anything went wrong.

The two rows of small metal tables pushed around the curved grey walls of the bar wouldn't provide any cover. But Jerico liked how people of all shapes, sizes and heights sat around the tables talking and laughing about their business. They were all drinking some kind of bright blue liquid that was probably strong enough to power small shuttles.

Jerico seriously didn't want to drink it if he could help it.

Jerico almost laughed as he saw three women in very attractive red dresses do some sort of exotic dancing on the oval platform in the middle of the bar. No one was paying attention to them so Jerico supposed their job was to simply get them in the bar.

But Jerico really didn't need them to get him in the bar.

Jerico went towards the massive bright red floating counter towards the very back of the bar. He clocked everyone was slowly looking at him, trying their best not to be seen, but he had been a Commander in the Imperial Army, he knew the signs of being watched. Jerico just needed to know how to find some forbidden information on a target and then he would leave all of these people in peace.

Most of them would hopefully be too drunk later on to remember him.

The closer he got to the counter the louder the humming, banging and popping of the space station got, it had faded as background noise so it was only now Jerico was realising the noise was still there. He still didn't like it, because it could easily hide the footsteps of enemies.

He gave the very tall woman behind the bar a friendly smile, but he was laughing more at himself than her. He just couldn't believe how obsessed he was with strategy and knowing how to win in a fight, he knew the skills were useful but they always popped up at weird times.

The woman smiled at Jerico as he leant against the icy coldness of the counter. The smells of oranges, lemons and grapefruits filled his senses making the great taste of lemon tarts form on his tongue.

"You want something that isn't alcohol, don't ya sweetheart?" the woman asked in a way that surprised Jerico. She sounded like she knew a lot more than Jerico wanted her to.

Jerico looked around the bar. All he wanted was a little information on where some human woman called Ithane Veilwalker could be, he had no idea what she really was. He was only going off what he had been told.

Jerico didn't believe for a single moment she was some woman who had been killed and brought back from the dead by some alien Goddess, but he had been gifted a task by a dying friend and he wanted to see it through.

"You seek someone," the woman said.

Jerico laughed and shook his head. He had no clue how to ask his question to this woman but he doubted she was as innocent or human as she appeared.

"I know if you want forbidden information then it is always best to start in the most remote regions of the Imperium," Jerico said keeping his voice as low as possible.

The woman smiled and nodded and Jerico looked around again and noticed a tall man wearing a black military uniform near the front door was watching them.

"Clearly I am not the only person who knows that little fact," Jerico said.

"Of course not," the woman said dropping her human-accent for just a moment.

Jerico took a step back and really looked at the woman. She looked so human with her thin waist, fat cheeks and long brown hair that she should be human.

But after a few moments, Jerico realised she was an alien Keres. He noticed how her ears might not have been pointed but they had been cut to remove the points, her waist was unnaturally thin and her facial features were all too perfect, too pointy, too human to be believable.

Jerico instantly wanted to reach for his pistol on his waist to protect her. Everyone in the Imperium knew to kill a Keres on site if they were found but Jerico couldn't allow that.

He had murdered way too many Keres over the decades out of blind obedience for him to let another human make the same mistakes he had.

Jerico leant very close to the Keres woman. "They will kill you if they find you,"

"I know," the woman said. "That is why the Man In Black is here. He had heard of magical miracles happening in this sector, I heal people you see who shouldn't be healed, so he came to investigate,"

"And now he wants to kill you," Jerico said hating the entire damn situation with the Imperium.

"If you help me escape then I promise you I will help you with whatever you need. Yet I need to know the topic,"

"I need to know where is Ithane Veilwalker?" Jerico asked, nodding.

The woman reached down below her counter and started to look like she was mixing drinks of some sort. Jerico really liked the intense aromas of orange and lemon and grapefruit but she was clearly acting.

The Man In Black was watching them intensely.

"Ithane Veilwalker is a myth created by your Imperium to give us false hope. The Keres are dying and we are being slaughtered by your Imperium. We want peace and you people enslave us,"

Jerico shook his head as he felt his necklace (that was apparently meant to contain the Soulstone of the Keres Goddess of Hope, Spero) pulse warmly around his neck.

Jerico took out the necklace and showed its bright blue jewel to the woman. "If that is a myth then why is Spero wanting me to find her?"

The woman's mouth dropped and Jerico could see she was conflicted and awed and even in a little fear as a drop of sweat rolled down her hand.

Then the woman laughed manically.

Jerico took a few steps back and whipped out his pistol.

The woman's veins turned black, black oil poured from her mouth and Jerico cursed under his breath. She was a Keres alright but she was a Dark Keres. She had sold her soul to the Keres God of Death Geneitor, a divine being devoted to the destruction of all life.

Or so the bullshit stories said.

Jerico aimed. He fired.

Bullets screamed through the air.

The woman laughed as she ate them and her arms transformed into immense black talons dripping dark red rich blood.

A scream came from behind.

Jerico spun around. He saw men and women run out of the bar screaming and shouting warnings as they went.

Space Station security would be there quickly. Jerico had to find his information soon.

The Black In Man charged at Jerico.

The woman flew forward.

Jerico rolled forward.

He fired at the Man.

The bullets bounced off him.

Jerico leapt up. The woman swung her talons at him.

Jerico blocked them. He punched her in the face.

Icy coldness shot up his arms.

The Man fired at the woman.

She screamed.

She shot out her arms. Black fire engulfed him.

He screamed in agony.

Jerico fired at the woman.

Tendrils of black fire melted the bullets but then the Man's screams just stopped and everything went silent.

When the silent flames finished crackling and engulfing the man, Jerico gasped as the Man was just a skeleton made from black crystal.

"Kill him," the woman said.

Jerico fired.

A bullet screamed towards the skeleton. It smashed into him. Shattering the crystal.

Jerico scanned the bar for the woman. She was gone.

He carefully searched behind the counter. He could sense her foul dark magic here. She was alive.

He just couldn't see her.

Jerico felt his heart pound in his chest. He felt sweat drip down his back. He could feel his fear responses kicking in.

Then Jerico's chest filled with the warmth of hope that Spero provided him with. He calmed down and he closed his eyes.

He wanted to sense the woman.

Air rushed behind him.

Jerico jumped forward. He opened his eyes.

He just missed two immense talons.

He fired into the air but he didn't hit anything.

Jerico closed his eyes again. He couldn't rely on human senses to find a Dark Keres. He had to rely on instinct.

Air zoomed towards him.

Jerico leapt to one side.

He felt the intense rush of heat flow past him. He wanted to panic at the idea of almost being cooked alive so he didn't allow himself to.

The air churned around him.

Jerico ducked. Fired three rounds all around him. He kicked the air.

He heard a scream as a bullet smashed into something and then his feet kicked the Keres's head.

Something cracked and Jerico opened his eyes to see the damn Keres woman collapse to the ground gripping her stomach as black blood poured out of the wound.

Jerico pointed his pistol firmly at her head but he was surprised that she was truly smiling at him. Her veins had returned to normal and Jerico had no idea how these Gods worked but he almost believed she had been freed of Geneitor's corrupting influence.

If such things actually happened.

"You helped me escape Geneitor. Thank you," the woman said weakly.

"Where is Ithane Veilwalker?" Jerico asked.

"The Father of Death knows. He tracks her but he only allows me to tell a lie and a truth before he claims my soul,"

"Speak and die then," Jerico said hating that he was being mean to a Keres that had probably only fallen to such corruption to survive humanity's onslaught.

"Ithane seeks the history of the Soulstones or Ithane can be found in the grave on Earth," the woman said before she died.

Jerico shook his head. It was clear that Ithane was alive, his old friend wouldn't have sent him on this mission if she could be found in a Grave so it was good to know he was looking for some History thing.

But Jerico just grinned to himself. His next task of following Ithane in her search for History was going to be next to impossible, everyone in the Imperium knew the Real History of everything was impossible to find.

The Rex had rewritten history thousands of thousands of times depending on what he wanted his human subjects to believe, so finding the True History of the Soulstones and anything related to the Keres was going to be next to impossible.

But as Jerico left the bar and looked for a shuttle to steal (ideally one that couldn't be traced), he was really excited for the future because this was going to be a hell of a mission and he truly loved impossible missions.

Especially when they involved hunting down impossible information and sorting fact from fiction in the crazy universe that was the Imperium.

INVASION OF THE LIBRARY OF LIFE

The thick aroma of smoke, charred flesh and death clung to the air as I leant against the icy cold white marble railing of the balcony I was using as my position. I, Ithane Veilwalker, enjoyed the small amounts of coldness flowing up my arms and into my soul.

The entire balcony itself was rather good for watching the surrounding forests considering it was a wide semi-circular marble platform used for academics, readers and other scholars. In normal times they would have read out here and studied their texts and ancient books in the bright sunlight.

That wasn't happening anymore.

I was completely alone on the balcony today and there weren't even any small crystal tables or chairs that had covered the balcony when I had first arrived a few days ago. There were still the little cuts, slices and chips in the floor where people had removed the tables and chairs, but they were so minor it hardly mattered.

The entire tower, or Library of Life as it was called by the locals, was a place I had always wanted to visit. The entire tower was created and handcrafted from a solid immense block of beautiful white marble with stunning gold veining coursing through it like a river.

I was even more impressed with the thousands of ancient leather-bound books that lined the white shiny shelves inside. I had never seen a real book before, most of them had been burnt and annihilated when the evil Rex had risen to power and conquered the Imperium.

Books really were special things to all of us remaining humans because we knew the key to our freedom and saving humanity was written in our past. The past that was burning down around us.

I smiled to myself as the taste of barbeques formed my tongue, my parents had always liked them with my siblings and our large family. They might have been all dead now but they had given me an amazing childhood.

A massive roar ripped through the air and I just shook my head as a bright red missile flashed through the sky smashing into the immense forest in the distance.

The sky was veiled in smoke, ash and little white pods called shuttles. I knew exactly why the Imperium was invading this world and killing my friends. They wanted to kill me and see what I knew about the Mother of Life.

I never realised that being resurrected by an alien goddess and being made into her Will incarnate would make me so popular with the monsters of the galaxy. But Genetrix wanted me on this world and thankfully I had a friend translating an ancient text for me now.

I felt Genetrix pull on my mind a little and I knew that I was running out of time. The Imperium would breach the world's defenders soon enough and then they would kill me and the knowledge of the text would be lost forever.

Of course I could easily open a portal and just leave but the text was too fragile to move and my damn translator wouldn't leave this planet. Some rubbish about their soul being bound to the world, I hated how magic worked at times.

"My Lady," someone said behind me.

I rolled my eyes as a Keres man came up to me. His alien humanoid features were perfectly thin, a little gaul and elongated. His body looked way too thin for a human but that was so common amongst the Keres.

Genetrix might have created the Keres to protect life and her evil husband might have created humanity to kill all life but they were basically the same in the looks department.

"Yes Tau'Koo," I said feeling Genetrix really trying to pull on my mind. There was something the

Goddess wanted me to realise but I just couldn't understand at the moment.

"The orbital defences are wiped out and the ground defenders are weaker now. The Imperium has landed in the North and South of the planet and Keres lives are being slaughtered,"

"Damn it," I said. I might have been 100% human with the powers of a Keres but I had never wanted the Keres to die. They were good, amazing people that had to be protected, but my presence had brought the enemy to them.

I needed a new plan.

"How much longer does the Translator need?" I asked.

"Another twenty minutes at least but which-"

I waved him silent because I knew exactly what was going to happen in the next twenty minutes, this world was going to die.

"Then let us see what power the Mother can gift me," I said closing my eyes and connecting to Genetrix and letting her presence feel my mind.

I tapped into her power and started to course over the immense forest below me with my mind's eye like how a bird might fly towards a seed on the ground. I needed to find the leader of the invasion and I needed to buy us time.

I found him.

I connected with his mind instantly. He wasn't a good man by any stretch of the imagination but he was skilled in hunting, killing and torturing Keres. I didn't need alien magic to realise that because I could sense the crystallised magic of his former kills.

Even now I was surprised that if the Keres were tortured for long enough their bodies would discharge their magic and connection to their patron God in an effort to save their life. It never worked but it didn't stop the biological processes of the Keres from doing it.

"I see you monster," I said echoing the words into his mind and hoping I could force a reaction of some kind.

I felt his thoughts turn happy that he actually wanted this and he had been expecting this.

"Where are you abomination?" he asked, "and tell me, what thoughts can you see?"

I didn't like it how he knew about the mind-reading ability Genetrix had gifted me. There had to be a spy amongst my gang and that was a major problem.

I didn't stop though, I could see his past and abuse from the family that was meant to love him. I could see how the Keres had robbed him of the chance to ever see if his parents could love him (they never were going to but he didn't realise that) and I could see his name.

He was Bloodheart.

The name almost forced me to kill the connection. Everyone in the galaxy knew who Bloodheart was, I wasn't even sure he was real or just a myth to keep the Imperium scared. He was a murderer, a butcherer and capable of burning an entire planet for the fun of the killing.

I only needed another 15 minutes.

"You are an impressive name to find Bloodheart," I said feeling Genetrix wanting me to leave.

But I couldn't. I could face Bloodheart.

"Do you realise that you are not the only human touched by the Keres Gods?" he asked. "There is another one of you and he is strong, deadly and will kill all life in this galaxy,"

I killed the connection as I felt something stand behind me.

I instantly went for the long magical sword at my waist but I felt a hard knife press against my back.

"Tau'koo," I said hardly impressed that the damn bastard actually had a blade at me.

"There are many within your ranks that do not agree having a human as the leader of the Daughters of Genetrix," Tau'Koo said.

I laughed because he was no Daughter of the Goddess, even I could hear the death, corruption and sickness in his voice. He was not devoted to life, he was the Deathbringer, a servant of Geneitor.

"When did the Father corrupt you?" I asked knowing I could kill him at a moment's notice but I just needed answers.

Immense booms ripped through the air. Huge

red flashes raced across the sky.

More missiles rained down on the planet. As did ten thousand little white pods. The ground forces were going to be overwhelmed in moments.

"The Father did not corrupt me. He showed me the truth about the galaxy and how humanity must die, the Keres must die, everyone must die,"

I snapped his neck with a single thought and whipped out my longsword as I went back into the immense library of Life. I was running out of time and I needed my answers.

I went along a narrow marble corridor with thousands of blue leather-bound books lining the shelves. None of them had been touched in decades but the hope of a better life and the magic within the pages kept the dust off them. Hope was a very powerful force in the galaxy.

After a few moments of going along the corridor, I just grinned as I ducked into a small white marble chamber through a small archway. There was a heavy wooden desk in the middle but my translator was dead.

Their body lumped over the damn desk and the ancient text was damaged.

I placed my hands on the translator's forehead, it was still warm and I hated the weird feeling of a warm dead body. It was wrong on so many levels.

"Let me see what never should be seen Mother of Life," I said quietly.

My mind was filled with curiosity, love and

happiness as I entered the translator's last final moments. At least they were happy with their last task for the Mother. They were reading a passage about a Soulstone and they were murdered.

I shook my head because it was the Soulstones I was after. Whoever collected all five shards of Genetrix's being could resurrect her and then she could finally kill her husband once and for all. It was simple and I needed to find all the Soulstones.

I sadly had to push my friend's corpse off the ancient book and their body turned to ash and I clicked my fingers so their soul went to the Mother instead of being tortured by the Father.

There was a bloody fingerprint highlighting one particular section and I couldn't read it. The language made no sense to me because I was a human, not a Keres and I didn't understand long lost languages.

But there was still a little bit of hope.

An immense boom ripped through the library and it sounded like a thousand tons of marble had just come smashing down.

I was seriously running out of time but the preservation of all life in the galaxy was more important than my single life.

I closed my eyes and tried to reconnect with the translator's passing soul but I couldn't. Once a soul was given to Genetrix she kept an iron grip on it.

I just couldn't help but laugh because this was so stupid and I couldn't possibly fail but Bloodheart was coming here. And I had seen in his mind when I connected only moments ago, he knew the ancient language and he knew exactly what I wanted with the Library.

"Return to me Bloodheart," I said as I reconnected with his mind.

I almost jumped as I didn't expect his mind to actually be in the Library. He was here stalking the halls and killing the Keres defenders as he went.

"I was waiting for you," he said, "because I wanted to show you a party trick,"

I screamed in agony as I was pulled through reality and dropped off in front of Bloodheart as him and me were completely alone in the ruined remains of a library.

The white marble walls were smashed and the smoke-veiled sky could easily be seen through the immense holes in the ceiling. There were plenty of Keres corpses littering the ground and I wanted to slaughter him right there and then.

There were even a few smashed marble pillars lining the edges of the library.

Bloodheart in his heavy, thick metal armour pointed his sword at my chest and aimed a pistol at my head.

I went a little cold as I felt my connection with Genetrix fade a little and I just realised that Bloodheart was a son of Geneitor. I had no idea how a human had fallen to the corruption but I was still so new at this.

"You will regret your choice of Patron," Bloodheart said. "The Father kills and he will enjoy you,"

"I regret nothing but why this world? I have been the Daughter of Genetrix for three months now. You have not attacked me in the void, on Ferum or five different worlds. Why this one?"

"Because this world has Keres on it. I love snapping the necks of the Keres as they sleep,"

"You are a monster," I said.

"I am what the galaxy has created me and I will help the Rex rule the stars in Humanity's name. No more Keres, no aliens, no more anything,"

I gasped for a moment as I realised Geneitor didn't have full control over him yet because Bloodheart still wanted humanity to live even though he had said the opposite only moments ago.

Bloodheart still had the weakness and mortality of a human.

He charged.

I thrusted out my hands.

Unleashing torrents of fire.

He flicked a wrist. My torrents went away.

He leapt into the air. Kicking me in the chest.

I fell backwards on the ground.

He landed on me. Kicking me again. Again.

The smell of death, smoke and rotting flesh filled my senses.

I shot out my hands.

Sending him backwards.

I shot up.

I flew at him.

Launching fireball after fireball.

He hissed.

He charged.

I charged.

We raised our swords.

We swung.

Our blades met.

Immense red flashes lit up the sky.

A missile screamed towards us.

I shot out another fireball.

Bloodheart hissed.

The missile smashed down on us.

I slammed my sword into the ground as the missile's explosive power was unleashed, I focused on my love for life, protecting the innocent and hope and a thin shield of dazzling white magical energy formed around me.

Bright flashes of gold, red and orange screamed past me as the deafening roar of an entire building collapsing echoed around me. I had failed the Mother, the Keres and ultimately humanity.

When the collapsing and the fire stopped, I closed my eyes and portalled myself to the top of the ruins where I simply sat on top of the very, very warm marble rubble. I didn't like how it was almost burning my bum but I didn't care because I was thankfully alive.

WAY OF THE ODYSSEY SHORT STORY COLLECTION
VOLUME 4

I hated how the sky was black with immense columns of black smoke veiling the sky. The forest was ablaze and all the little white pods were zooming back up into orbit because they had done their mission and I didn't doubt for a second that Bloodheart was alive.

The only sound of the entire planet now was the constant roaring, crackling and snapping of fires as they devoured all in their path. If there were members of the Dark Keres Cult on the planet then I wouldn't have been surprised if Geneitor was powering the life-destroying flames but thankfully they weren't here.

I just shook my head as I couldn't believe I had completely failed in my mission, then I felt my connection to the Mother restore itself and it felt happy.

A strange joy filled me as I realised that I wasn't just a human now constrained by the limits of a human mind. I was also a Keres with the power of a Goddess behind me, and I started to remember little passages and shards of information from the section of ancient text I had been reading earlier, that was all me.

But I understood it now and I just laughed as I realised my magic must have coursed its way through Bloodheart's mind when we were fighting and it must have found where he kept all his information about the Keres ancient language.

The passage the Translator wanted me to understand was that the Soulstones might have been bought together at one point in history. It was after all the ritual that tried to resurrect Genetrix failing at the same exact time as my own death that brought around my creation.

It was still more than that though, the book was mentioning how the Soulstones never wanted to be apart from each other and they wanted to be found. They would influence the environments, the worlds, the cultures that surrounded them so someone would eventually notice something was seriously wrong in a good or bad way.

I just shook my head because this was basically asking me to understand how the Soulstones had been discovered in the first place and then I could look for similar signs in the present. But the galaxy was a massive place, filled with billions of different planets and a Soulstone could be on any one of them.

I stood up and took a final look at this now-dead world I could sense that a darkness was coming here. Geneitor had a world to consume and he had a lot of dead souls to collect, but I was never going to allow him that for I might be a human but I am Ithane Veilwalker, Daughter of Genetrix and I am a protector of life.

I clicked my fingers and felt my connection with Genetrix strengthen as I collected all the souls on the planets and gifted them to her.

Then I swirled, twirled and whirled my arms

about and I opened a bright golden portal to my flagship with my cult. I had a lot of reading to do, a lot of learning and a lot of things to think about because I was making progress and that was a wonderful feeling to have.

One day Genetrix would rise once more and then the entire galaxy would know the meaning of life and death. And only one side would win forever.

AMONGST THE ENEMY

This was the day I died.

I, Intelligence Officer Isaac Oldman, sat in the middle of an icy cold purple prison cell made from pure crystal. The prison cell wasn't too ugly, in fact it definitely had a certain beauty about it that I was shocked about.

I really enjoyed watching little creatures or whatever the foul alien Keres put into their magic crystals, as they pulsed, swirled and twirled around inside the stunning crystal. It was rather hypnotic in a strange way.

The prison cell itself wasn't much bigger than me but that was the strange thing about Keres technology, it very much had an evil mind of its own. If I wanted to stand up, the prison cell would get larger, if I wanted to sit down the entire cell would get a hell of a lot smaller. It was creepy that way and the sheer darkness of the purple crystal didn't allow me to see anything outside.

Thankfully I was an intelligence officer from the Imperial Secret Service so I was used to travelling beyond the holy realm of the Imperium and traveling into the darkness and coldness and foulness of the galaxy outside. It was only two years ago I was inside the so-called Enlightened Republic, the foul breakaway regions that were building nuclear weapons to destroy the Imperium once and for all.

All whilst they pretended to build a traitorous democracy. As if humans could actually rule themselves without the Rex's guiding light. It was just laughable.

But I knew how the foul Keres worked so I was probably stuck on some Rex-forsaken moon with thousands of other prisoners. Yet unlike me those other prisoners were probably not righteous, for only humanity would rule the stars and soon humanity would annihilate the Keres once and for all.

And then their evil magic could be erased from the universe.

Maybe I should have given the Keres more credit though, I was basically naked at this point with only a thin purple sheet around me. I had no doubt it was covered in magic and the foul aliens were searching my mind, thankfully my training had covered those stupid basics so the Keres were never going to get my secrets.

The air was sweet and filled with hints of grapes, grapefruit and blood oranges. Yet knowing exactly how evil these aliens were they were probably the smells of their own kind that they were sacrificing to their own gods and goddesses, the Keres were beasts at heart.

At least the sweet smells left the great taste of fruit salad on my tongue exactly how my mother used to make it.

The sweet aromas got even stronger and I hated myself for daring to confirm the thoughts of the weird magic of the Keres. They were probably wanting to lure me into their mind games using smells but I was a human, I was righteous, I wouldn't be tempted by their witchery.

In fact I was just glad that I was okay and I sent off all my information to the wonderful Imperial authorities before these beasts captured me.

At least now the Imperium had a fighting chance against the awful predations of the Keres.

Let me tell you exactly what I sent them.
***

+++Transmission Recording+++

Dear Lord Eraser,

Apologies for the lateness of my call but these beasts are far more intelligent than we ever gave them credit for, they know what humans are and they actively hunt them down. We need to exterminate them as soon as possible, and how the hell we didn't annihilate them after the Great War is beyond me.

I am not questioning His wisdom just the consequences of the action.

I am currently laying on top of an immense purple crystal rooftop on top of the Keres version of a holy skyscraper. I have to admit I am more than impressed with the sheer straightness, perfection and smoothness of the sides of the building.

I had no idea creatures could make such a building out of pure purple crystal. This seems to be the location of where the Keres live, they create vast purple cities filled with these skyscrapers to live in.

At some point I might seek to gain entrance into these abominable buildings but I must be patient my Lord. I know the Keres might be tracking my transmission so by the Rex I must be careful.

For as far as I can see the buildings rise up like immense purple daggers veiling the sky, ground and mountains like each hab-block (though I doubt that is what these monsters call their buildings) are like fortifications. I will seek to access their weakness so if an attack is needed we can bomb them in their sleep.

Which thankfully my Lord I can confirm the Keres do need. It is currently midnight on the planet and there is much less traffic about. The bright purple metal pods that the Keres use as transports are far fewer right now than they were earlier. You should have seen them my Lord, it was disgusting, huge purple streaks of pods through the sky.

It was an abomination to humanity's birthright and was nothing compared to the holy whiteness of our shuttles. It makes me sick just mentally sending this to you.

The air stinks, my lord, of foul oranges, grapefruits and grapes. This I must investigate further to make sure this is a food source and not some kind of biological weaponry, but I will confess the sheer silence of the city concerns me greatly.

There are no sounds of their awful high-pitched language, no shuttles zooming about the rest. This is most unnatural and I will admit my fear of exploring this most alien of worlds is building.

I will continue my mission for the Rex.

+++Transmission Send+++

***

+++Transmission Signal Searching+++
+++Transmission Signal Found and Sending+++

Immense bangs, pops and explosions echo around me my Lord as I enter a huge purple crystal "factory". That is what this place must be because it is so different to all the other types of buildings I have explored so far.

This building like all the others is simply made from living purple crystal with little strange lights that pulse, swirl and twirl around inside. I feel like they are looking at me half the time and I hate these creatures, I hate aliens and I can feel the cold fearful sweat drop down my back.

I am a warrior my Lord. I am not a recon specialist but I do not seek to question the Rex.

The "factory" was amazing as I watched the long lines of purple crystals, metals and corpses float up in the cold air in long, long lines high above me. If any of those corpses were still alive then I would probably look like some random ant or something.

The factory was so huge and I was so tiny.

Yet it was the silence that still infuriated me. I was used to so much sound, so much noise, so much joy but I couldn't hear anything.

So I did the only logical thing my Lord and I followed the endlessly long lines for as long as I could. I followed it to a large purple crystal balcony that overlooked a stunning pit of some sort.

I was amazed at it because the Keres were here. So many evil, corrupt, demonic Keres were here and I had a weapon on me, but I had to focus on the mission.

Recon only.

All the evil Keres were so thin with their tiny waists, largeish chests and sharp pointy humanoid features that it was simply disgusting, and a perversion of the Rex's divine Will. It was disgraceful that these aliens ever believed the Rex would allow them to look so close to humans.

I studied the females in their long black dresses that swept across the floor with long blond pieces of hair floating up like the air and constantly moving, almost like they were scanning the air.

I just hoped these creatures weren't intelligent enough to detect me.

The Keres stood in their long lines and as soon

as a shard of crystal, a chunk of metal and a chunk of a corpse floated past, they would simply click their fingers and in a bright flash of magical light they would become weapons.

I saw guns, rocket launchers and laser swords being created.

And by the Rex did this annoy me. These Keres actually dared to create arms, armour and evil weapons against the righteousness of humanity that was disgusting and I wanted nothing more than to simply slaughter them all.

This was in direct violation of the Treaty of Defeat that these pathetic creatures signed after they lost the war.

Then everything stopped.

All the Keres looked directly at me.

They thrusted out their hands.

Magical fireballs zoomed towards me.

I ran like hell.

The enemy knew I was here.

+++Transmission sent+++

***

+++Transmission Sending+++

Dear Lord Eraser,

I need an urgent evacuation and urgent military reinforcements sent to my location immediately. The problem is far, far worse than I ever could have imagined.

The Keres were more demonic than we ever thought possible.

After the Keres started to hunt me down, I managed to escape into some kind of sewage network and it was mightily impressive because all the waste created by this society is simply magically teleported down into the sewer tunnels and they end up into a conversion chamber.

Then magic turns the waste into something useful again.

Of course I had to kill three foul Keres males to get you that information but it was worth it, and the entire Keres race will hopefully burn for it.

Anyway my Lord, after I escaped I knew the Keres were going to use their abominable magic to hunt me down so I decided to invade their homes, learn some more information and hopefully learn a secret to their undoing.

Let me tell you my Lord, our reports and beliefs and information about the Keres living like plebs couldn't be further from the truth.

I'm currently leaning against a bright purple wall made of pure crystal in some of the apartments and every single apartment is open concept, open plan and open everything. I do not believe these creatures even know what a door is.

Instead of sofas, they had a strange orange floating thing in front of a row of pink diamonds, which I now believe is a type of communication network using their magic to power it all.

I tried to get the young Keres woman to show

how it worked but she refused, so I killed her.

The kitchen area is even stranger my Lord, because there are no holo-freezers, holo-ovens or even a food synthesiser. There are just bowls of huge blue melons and I think the Keres just magic up their food and drink.

That is what another young man was doing before I stormed in and killed him.

It is no wonder these aliens are so dumb and inferior to humanity. Maybe these lazy aliens learnt how to cook instead of filling their bodies with magic then maybe their species wouldn't be as braindead as humanity.

Thankfully that just makes killing them easier.

But my biggest concern is the massive bright orange, glowing sack on the bright white ceiling. It concerns me because I believe there were small, baby Keres inside.

Every so often when the bright orange sack flashes, I can see small fingers, small legs and small faces just staring me at smiling, laughing and waiting for something bad to happen.

Of course I would never kill these baby Keres because that is not what the Rex wants. He requires baby Keres to be indoctrinated into the ways of humanity so they see their own species as corrupt and evil, and in the end the Keres will annihilate themselves and become slaves for humanity.

That is why the Rex is so clever because he is always so much further ahead of the enemy.

But this concerns me greatly because all these apartments that I have broken into have these orange sacks above them. I don't like this and this means that instead of the Keres population dying off like we believed.

It was actually growing and that means the Keres will soon be able to raise an army against us.

We must be ready.

Someone's coming.

+++Transmission sent+++

***

I have to admit I didn't expect the Keres to simply click their fingers and knock me out when one of their military commanders in their golden, ornate armour stormed and took me prisoner.

I just stared at the bright white lights flashing about in my purple prison cell as I realised that I shouldn't have been able to remember those things. I was an intelligence officer and my mind was a fortress and once I did something in the Rex's name I shouldn't have been able to remember it, much less recall it inside an enemy prison.

A sweet musical laughter echoed all around me as the purple drained away from the crystal to become see-through. I just frowned as I saw I was isolated in the middle of nowhere on some damn moon.

For as far as I could see there was only endless amounts of grey rock, there were no people, no signs of life and no other signs of prisoners. There was just me alone and I knew I was about to die.

I had read a lot of intelligence reports over the years and I knew how the immoral Keres worked. As soon as the crystal prison cell went away I would choke to death and I wouldn't be able to scream.

There would be no air at all.

The sweet aromas of blood oranges, grapefruit and grapes went away to be replaced with the cold smell of dust. Because in the end that was all what the galaxy was, one single massive sheet of dust, rock and death.

"Thank you for revealing your mind to me," a human woman said into my mind.

"I did not reveal anything to you, and why do you work for the Keres? If this is mental conditioning then fight back, fight for humanity, fight for the Rex," I said with authority.

The woman laughed inside my mind. "You are a fool little man because the Keres are innocent creatures that humanity were scared of. We slaughtered their race for nothing except fear and now I am making things right by helping them,"

"Traitor. Murderer. Evil woman,"

"Call me whatever you want but I know the truth Isaac and I know what is coming for humanity and the Keres. A force so great that only the Goddess Genitrix can save us,"

I just laughed at the stupidity of this woman, clearly she had fallen for the delusional ideology and mythology of the Keres. The idea that the Big Bang was caused by the birth of a Goddess of Life and a God of Death and the Keres were created to guard life and humanity was born to destroy all life and serve the God of Death.

It was stupid and I honestly pitied this pathetic woman.

"You can never change so I will release you from your fleshy body and I just pray to Genetrix that she grabs your soul before He does,"

I was about to protest out loud when I noticed the crystal prison cell was gone and I could no longer breathe.

"And thank you for the transmissions," the woman said. "They never reached the Imperium and I will always fight against your corrupt oppressive empire,"

My eyes just widened in horror as I collapsed gasping for air that wasn't there and I just hoped that the Keres would all die out because they were evil, I had seen that first-hand and I bore witness to their foulness because I had lived amongst the enemy.

And now I could happily die for my sins.

CORRUPTING DARKNESS

Thick choking aromas of smoke, charred flesh and boiling blood filled Captain Henry Oblong's senses as his eyes slowly flickered open. He had no idea where he was, how he had gotten here or what was actually happening.

All he could do was focus on the terrible, ugly, awful smell that seemed to fill the air like the evil cousin of oxygen was trying to replace it. Henry coughed and he just wanted to be okay. He hated the foul taste of charred flesh that formed on his tongue.

Henry didn't want to be on some strange alien world. He wanted to be protecting humanity, saving people's lives and just helping to make sure humanity lasted one day at a time in this cold deadly galaxy.

He slowly tried to move his hands side to side to feel what he was on or at least touching, he was surprised by the sheer icy coldness of the sandy ground beneath him. He realised he was on his back, winded and he was struggling to breathe.

Henry really tried to remember why the hell he was here. He was an Imperial soldier he knew that, he had enlisted when he was 16 to make sure that humanity was protected against the traitors, aliens and the so-called magic that certain alien races were corrupted by.

Henry had no idea at all why he was on his back on a planet filled with such an awful atmosphere. It was so disgusting that he actually wanted to be sick but real soldiers do not vomit. That was the golden rule of the Imperium.

After a few more seconds of choking and struggling to breathe, Henry forced himself up and he really focused on his surroundings.

He was surprised that there was nothing around him except the burning, crackling and popping wreckage of bright a white pod that he had been travelling in. Henry was meant to meet up with a massive Imperial fleet that was gathering in the area to scourge the aliens off these worlds.

As much as Henry wanted to go over to the pod, he sadly knew there was nothing he could do now. The pod was destroyed and Henry guessed it was hardly natural for an Imperial pod to get blown out the sky. It was probably shot, bombed or maybe some foul magic had forced it to land.

Henry hated aliens and he was going to kill them all in the end.

Henry forced his attention away from the pod

and hated the sheer thickness of the black smoke that swirled, twirled and whirled around him. It didn't seem natural because there wasn't any wind, there were no forces at play here to explain what he was seeing and Henry didn't like how he felt like he was being watched.

The coldness of the air made him shiver and Henry realised that unless he made it to shelter or something soon. He was going to die and then humanity had one less soldier to defend itself with. Something he absolutely couldn't allow.

Henry forced himself to take a step forward then another then another.

Henry felt like he was swimming through pea soup or something just as harsh, cold and evil. He had thankfully heard and studied and killed more magical aliens, Keres, than he cared to think about but this wasn't their style.

The Keres were a dying out alien race that were weak, pathetic and evil down to their very core. Yet their pathetic-ness made them cowards at heart so they were all about ambushing and this wasn't ambushing.

Henry could have sworn he saw shadows and figures move in the darkness of the smoke but as soon as he blinked they were gone. The smoke burnt his eyes and caused water to stream down his face this was a nightmare and he hated every single minute of it.

He felt around for his gun, knife and pistol that he always carried on his waist but they were gone. Henry swore under his breath as he forced himself to continue.

If the enemy had shot him down then there was no telling what he was dealing with so the only ally he had here was higher ground so he could hopefully get out of this damn smoke.

Then he took a step that changed everything.

Henry stepped forward and jerked himself as he no longer felt sand under his feet but something hard and shiny and awful as he found himself in a brand-new black crystal chamber.

He had no clue what had just happened but this was bad. The chamber was large made from shiny black crystal that pulsed with blood red energy and Henry felt like he was meant to touch it.

He knew that would be a bad idea if there ever was one.

The air stunk of charred flesh, ash and death as Henry paced around hoping for a way out of the chamber but there wasn't one.

The domed ceiling made from shiny black crystal was even brighter with blood red energy than the sides, and Henry really wanted to escape.

The crystal walls of the prison hummed, vibrated and banged. Henry broke into a fighting stance and then he swore the foul aliens that he had never thought he would see behind this most unholy act against humanity.

Out of the crystal walls a single very tall and scarily thin humanoid female stepped out. Blood red energy glowed on her pale white skin and face and body where veins and arties should have been.

Henry just focused on the female's pointy, sharp face that he was fairly sure could be used as a weapon in its own right. She was a Keres but definitely not one of the aliens he had seen before.

The female swirled her hand and red magical energy made the air crackle as she smiled.

"Captain Henry," the female said, her human tongue harsh, unrefined and just plain awful.

Henry wanted to kill her there and then. All the foul Keres knew that under the Treaty of Defeat attacking humanity was the worst possible crime, punishable by extermination.

Of course humanity was allowed to kill the Keres as they pleased but if the Keres were less bestial then they might have won the war instead of being defeated like the pathetic creatures they were.

"I was excited to meet such a kill like yourself," the female said her voice becoming more and more of an echo. "I had wondered by the glory of Geneitor would make our paths cross,"

Henry just rolled his eyes. It was beyond pathetic of the Keres to believe in their flawed and unholy mythology about how a God called Geneitor had created death and sought to kill all life but the Mother of Creation Genetrix sought to protect it.

"Release me demon," Henry said. "Your race is breaking the law and I will burn you for it,"

The female smiled. "Then my species does not have much of an incentive to do that, does it? And I have much more important uses for you in the services of Geneitor,"

"I will never turn, I will never reveal secrets and I will always protect humanity,"

The female laughed. "Every single human says that when I capture them but they always turn,"

"I am not a normal human," Henry said. "I am a soldier, a hero of humanity and I am a killer of the Keres,"

The female shivered in pleasure and Henry wanted to be sick.

"His Lordship is grateful for the souls of the murdered so thank you. They keep him powerful, stirring and strong enough to one day return to this dying galaxy so he can complete what the foul Mother stopped him from doing," she said.

Henry shook his head.

He charged.

The female clicked her fingers and Henry froze. He tried to fight, scream, kick. He couldn't do anything.

"Humans are always so inelegant and you haven't asked me who I am," the female said. "My name is The Corrupter, a champion of Geneitor and it is my job to corrupt the souls of Keres and humans alike so they may serve him even in death,"

Henry laughed. He had never heard of such rubbish in all his life.

"Let us take a little trip around my encampment,"

Before Henry could ever think about protesting, choking blood red smoke engulfed him and he felt the world fall away from him.

***

Henry was hardly impressed with the stupid Corrupter as he found himself alone standing in the middle of a massive group of skin-crafted tents with a roaring, crackling fire in the middle.

He had to admit that tents were domed, ugly and Henry realised he didn't need to have magic to know that they were crafted out of human skin, there was even some blood and muscle still attached to some sheets of skin flapping about in the coldness of the air.

He enjoyed the scents of flowers, jasmine and chilli in the air before it was leaving replaced with the foul scent of charred flesh that was so strong in the air he was almost choking. He hated the Keres.

The flames of the fire danced a little and a moment later the Corrupter appeared smiling at him in fiery form.

"It is amazing that you believe we are Keres, but we are Dark Keres, Fallen Keres or Shadow Walkers depending on what idiots you ask about us," the Corrupter said.

"Why bring me here? Why not just kill me and let your false God feast on my soul?" Henry asked knowing that Geneitor was nothing more than a myth created by a dying alien race.

The Corrupter laughed. "Look around you Captain Henry,"

Henry nodded as he stared at the skin-crafted tents and how cold, unloved and isolated each of them looked. Then he saw long feral claws were reaching out of the tents.

"This is what I have had to do to save Keres race. Souls keep Geneitor alive long enough for his influence to spread but the Great War must be fought and the Keres race must be saved,"

"What are you talking about? Your race is an abomination that deserves to die," Henry said.

Henry walked round to the other side of the fire and he was surprised that not a single hint of warmth came from it.

"When humanity attacked my home planet, burnt my village, killed my entire family. I escaped into the Ultraspace network, you know that intergalactic transport system you stole from us,"

Henry smiled. That was definitely one of the greatest benefits of the war and it was so worth all the bloodshed that righteous humanity had committed.

"I was about to die in the network when Geneitor found me, he convinced me to serve him and he shared some of his power with me. He gave me the secret to destroying humanity and saving the

Keres race,"

Henry shook his head. These aliens deserved to die and there was nothing she could say that would convince him otherwise.

"I need to find the Stones of Geneitor and bring him into this universe so we can wipe out humanity once and for all. Then my race can be safe again with the God of Death looking over us,"

Henry spat at her. "If your God is so powerful then why can my species kill you all so easily,"

"The Dark Keres are outcasts, hunted by the mainstream Keres in case humanity learn about us and wage war against us once more. The Keres are scared and look at what the Dark Keres have been reduced to,"

Henry didn't care that these aliens had been reduced to living out of skin-crafted tents, forced to eat corpse meat off the bone judging by the bones littering the campsite, and he really didn't care the Dark Keres were weak.

"You are a dying race and that is it," Henry said. "You cannot make anything, you cannot protect yourself, you cannot do anything,"

The Corrupter sighed. "That is all true and we have no need for money or trade because the gifts of the Destroyer but I was hoping to turn you more easily but watch what I show you next. This is the truth,"

Henry was about to protest when his mind

started to fill with images of dying humans, men and women just being murdered by other humans. There were images of corruption and evil bargains being struck in the highest levels of Imperial Government and more images revealed the creation of super weapons.

Henry knew they were being created to be used against the Enlightened Republic, the stupid breakaway regions of humanity that believed in democracy against the righteous control of the Rex.

So many innocent humans would be destroyed simply because they chose democracy over the Rex. That was wrong and Henry didn't want that.

The people of the Enlightened Republic needed to be sent to re-education camps not killed.

"Geneitor could save them all," The Corrupter said. "You once mentioned to a friend that your purpose is to save humanity, protect it and keep innocent people alive,"

Henry nodded that was the entire point of his being.

"If you join Geneitor I can promise you that these people will be saved, protected and live alongside the Keres. The Republic has no problem with my race so they will not be killed,"

Henry had to agree with her there. He knew the Imperium would wipe out all non-Imperial fractions sooner or later that meant a lot of innocent people dying.

Henry looked at the Corrupter. "Are there such

things as innocent Keres?"

The Corrupter stepped out of fire returning to her flesh and blood form. Her pale white face smiling at him.

"Me and Geneitor can promise you that the Keres did not start this war. Humanity was scared of our power and that made them shoot first,"

Henry felt something start to press against his mind. It felt so pleasurable, calming and safe like it was a parent offering him a hug, maybe the Keres were not so bad after all and if humanity was capable of so much murder and bloodshed then maybe they did need to be stopped with Genitor's help.

That way he could continue to help humanity, save lives and just protect every single human he had always wanted to do ever since he was 16 years old.

"What will happen to me when I convert?" Henry asked.

The Corrupter smiled and hugged him. "Nothing bad. You will simply accept Geneitor into your heart, mind and body. You will become stronger, tougher and see the universe in a brand-new way,"

Henry nodded. It sounded scary as hell but he had to protect humanity no matter the cost.

"But I will warn you if you choose this path then humanity will hunt you down, mainstream Keres will hunt you down and so will the Daughters of Generatrix. Is that a risk you would want to take?"

Henry nodded.

The Corrupter smiled and Henry's mind exploded as he became a Dark Keres.

***

Six months later, Henry smiled as he stood on a massive desert planet covered in golden sand for as far as the eye could see. There were no dunes, no hills nor mountains but Henry was more than glad about that. It meant there were basically no places for the evil humans to run away to.

The air stunk of jasmine, flowers and mint that left the great taste of mint ice cream form on his tongue. He had no idea why the humans had choked and coughed and hissed in pain as they breathed in the air but that was the stupid thing about humans they just didn't know what was good for them.

Henry gripped his bone spear tightly as his fellow Keres came over to him. They all looked so great, angelic and beautiful with their long claws, bone spikes shooting out of their armour and their long fangs looked perfect as they dripped small amounts of blood onto the ground.

Henry still couldn't believe it had taken so long for him to accept Genitor's gifts because that was the thing about the Destroyer, he was never a bad man, he didn't destroy people's minds. He only gave them the tools to realise that the galaxy was an evil place and humanity was the greatest challenge they faced.

Humanity had to die to make sure the Keres survived and that was all that mattered.

Henry licked his fangs with his hard snake

tongue as he looked forward to hunting down the rest of the humans on the planet and sacrifice their fat juicy souls to Genitor and hopefully some of them would even see the enlightenment that the Destroyer had offered him.

Humanity was going to pay for their sin of existence and Henry had no problem with that at all.

It was going to be a beautifully dark and bloody future, exactly what the God of Death wanted and Henry didn't want to disappoint his Lord and Master. Not for a single second.

ASHES OF VALICAN

An entire world was burnt to ash in a matter of minutes.

When I, Elizabeth Sobeth, was summoned to investigate the events of Valican, I hardly doubted it was anything more than a simple case of a planet being miscategorised by the idiots of the Imperium and their so-called divine Rex.

What I actually found terrified me.

According to scans, maps and a number of highly rated travel books, I should have been standing in the middle of a luscious ocean with amazing colourful fish, monsters and tourists would come here for months at a time to sail on these stunning seas.

Believe me that couldn't be further from the truth because I was standing in the middle of an ash-covered stretch of land that really did go on endlessly for miles upon miles. There was nothing here for ash that was constantly getting blown up and kicked into the air by a harsh warm breeze.

The ash was an interesting mixture of black, grey and yellow that constantly swirled around each other in weird alien ways that I didn't understand.

I wanted to believe it was nothing more than damage from a massive fire but considering that there were no signs of life, no signs of water and no signs of anything on the planet, I knew I was just hoping for the impossible. Something or a group of people had killed an entire planet.

Thankfully, after I made my full report to Earth and the Rex himself, this would all be out of my hands. Because the very last thing that I wanted to do was deal with a group of aliens or humans that had the power to burn an entire world.

The sheer smell of ash, smoke and charred flesh filled my senses and clawed at my lungs. I wished I had bought my damn rebreather but that was impossible because I had left it on my black ship in orbit.

Something that I really didn't like about the planet besides the smell and walking on ash, was the sheer silence of the planet.

I had read the reports and documents in Imperial Records and this entire planet had hosted over two billion humans, it was a fairly advanced colony and the people were making a killing off the tourism trade.

So who could have done the annihilation of an entire planet so easily? There wasn't a call for help, any survivors or any sign that anyone knew what was happening.

I went off into the distance, hating how soft and crumbly the ash-covered ground felt under my feet and my stomach twisted in a painful knot at the idea of the ash collapsing and me falling into a pit.

That was a very real fear.

The sky was remarkably clear considering the sheer amount of ash on the ground. The sun was shining brightly off the intensely light ash so I was more than happy I was wearing a holo-visor, protecting my eyes from the intense UV light, and my robes were long so I shouldn't burn.

Yet I feared that burning and going blind were the least of my problems.

I kept walking through the ash covered wastelands, just hoping that I would find something to tell me what had happened.

I always carried a small black box device that allowed me to take air and ash samples but I had done that earlier. The air was perfectly okay and the oxygen levels seemed to be increasing oddly enough despite the lack of trees on Valican.

"Do you know me?" a voice said behind me.

I stopped instantly because no one was there a minute ago so I turned around and jumped.

A woman was sitting there.

I just focused on the tall, very thin woman just sitting there like she was dying or something. I knew she was from the planet because she was wearing the traditional long white robes of this culture and golden rings were wrapped around her neck. One for each of the so-called Great Beasts she had killed.

Apparently on Valican there were ten Beasts that a person needed to kill to be ruler of the planet. The Rex had always found that detail funny so he allowed the humans to continue that weird tradition even under his tyrannical rule.

And yes I do realise everything I have already said in this report is more than enough to get me executed for treason against the Rex. But oh well.

The woman had nine of the rings around her neck and her face was smiling but her lips were cracked and her eyes were glassy. She was blind and she was looking right at me.

And I could have sworn she was staring into my soul.

"I don't know you," I said. "I am Doctor Elizabeth of the Imperial Science Division,"

"Are you here about the monsters and the Space Children?" the woman asked.

I hated how I had to remember every single little detail about this weird culture. She knew that the Rex normally burnt worlds for believing in any being besides him but this world had humoured him for some reason.

I wish my own home planet was that lucky.

"What are the Star Children?" I asked.

"The creatures you call the Keres that came down from the skies in screaming pods of purple, black and blue. They howled and roared and screamed bloody murder in the name of their dark God Geneitor," the woman said.

Valican grabbed her stomach. She felt it knot and churn violently. She had faced the Dark Keres before, magical alien beings that wanted to resurrect their God of Death so he could wipe out humanity and save the Keres race from annihilation.

Annihilation that humanity had unjustly started. Again that simple sentence would so get me murdered by the Rex.

"What happened here?" I asked kneeling down on the ash-covered ground so I was at least eye-level with the woman. She followed my gaze perfectly.

It was so creepy.

"We were all just minding our own business. I was feeding young girls in the market and listening to them talking about dates they were going on later tonight. That is when the sun went out for a minute as the pods of the Dark Keres screamed out,"

I jerked backwards slightly because this woman wasn't what she was pretending to be, because not a single human outside of the highest levels of Imperial government and rarely the Imperial Army knew there was a difference between the Dark Keres, Keres and the Daughters of Generatrix. Another offshoot of the Keres race that wanted to resurrect their Goddess of Life to safeguard the Keres race.

"Who are you?" I asked.

The woman grinned. "A trickster some say. A monster others say. What do you call me Doctor

Sobeth?"

She knew who I was. That couldn't be possible and that was just wrong on so many levels.

"You want to tell me what you and your people did to this world," I said knowing this foul alien probably wanted to kill me as much as I wanted to kill it.

"We needed souls for Geneitor. He was hungry and our warband was interested in burning a world for the fun of it and we wanted to unleash the Incarnation,"

I shivered at the very mention of the Incarnation. I had heard it mentioned a lot of times in hushed voices when I was serving alongside a detachment of Imperial special forces.

No one had ever seen the creatures but the rumours were powerful enough. It was said that once there were enough murders, spilled blood and screams on a battlefield that The Champion of Death could summon a shard of Geneitor's soul into the galaxy.

In the form of a demonic monster known as the Incarnation. A creature so powerful, monstrous and deadly that entire armies could explode in minutes.

"Did you summon him?" I asked really knowing I had to find a way to kill this woman before she killed me.

"No," the woman said sounding disappointed. "That was not what caused the death of your world.

The death of your world was more sudden than a simple battle and I know the Dark Keres were not behind it,"

I shook my head. She had to be lying. The Dark Keres had attacked this innocent human world so the killers had to be them. Right?

"You are a clever soul Doctor. You know I can sense Geneitor wanted to lick and taste your soul so you will be killed at some point. I know that would make my Master happy but you must look closer to home to find out who had murdered your people,"

She charged.

Jumping on me.

She punched me.

Fangs shot out of her.

I gripped her fangs.

They glowed blood red.

Burning my hands.

I snapped them.

Thrusting them into the woman's head.

The woman laughed loudly as I killed her and I kept stabbing her until she didn't laugh anymore.

But if what she said was true then I needed to return to my ship and research if the Imperium had ordered this murder.

And if the Dark Keres had simply come here to feast on the souls because they knew the humans were already going to die.

***

As much as I didn't like my small, cramped

research ship that was nothing more than a black circular sphere with only one room in the entire ship, I had to admit that it did have excellent research capabilities.

I sat in a giant black metal chair holding a small holo-reader as I scanned Imperial archives of what had happened to Valican over its lifetime and what top-secret projects were rumoured to live here.

The rest of the ship was only the size of a swimming pool but it was filled with so many holo-readers, pieces of research equipment and food containers because I wasn't allowed a food synthesiser there was barely any room left for me.

I hated the ship almost as much as I hated the Rex himself.

Anyway, the archives showed that Valican was once a death world because it was so far away from the sun that it couldn't possibly support any forms of life. Yet these are exactly the sort of worlds that the Dark Keres love to hide on.

When Valican was first encountered by Imperial forces, they found two warbands of Dark Keres on the surface, so they were murdered and the planet suddenly became filled with trees, animals and oceans.

At the time no one cared because this was right after the Treaty of Defeat was signed so the Keres race had lost the war, humanity was basically subtly enslaving them and the human race was safe whilst they continued to murder a peaceful species.

But I now believe this was a trick done by the being known as Geneitor to lure humans to the world so he could kill them at a later date.

I had to sadly readjust myself in my metal chair because the icy coldness of space was seeping more and more into my ship. That meant the damn heater and engine systems were failing.

I didn't have long left to discover the truth before I had to flee and stop my search.

However, as much as I like that theory I have to admit it is wrong. Since the problem with Imperial Records on Geneitor is even though I have heard rumours of the Rex acknowledging the existence of the Keres God and Goddess he refuses to allow research on them so the majority of humanity did not fall to their corrupting influence.

I sort of understand that.

Anyway, the small amount of data I can find about Geneitor is that he never ever creates life. He only kills it so the idea he could create an entire planet filled with trees just to lure in humans seemed impossible.

So I believe humanity used a terraforming technology that was not documented and that led to the creation of Valican.

A much more likely theory has to come from the Lord Planetary Governor of Valican himself because before he was assassinated and the Rex himself directly ruled over the planet, he confessed to a series of nuclear experiments.

Since the Planetary Governor wanted to learn why and how humanity had almost annihilated Earth before using this technology. And as much as the Rex's supporters claimed the ruler of humanity cleared out the planet of nuclear waste, I know the Rex would never do that.

A weapon is a weapon and nuclear weapons would be like the best present ever to the Rex.

There's no way in hell he destroyed them so there is a good chance these nuclear weapons went off during the attack of the Dark Keres.

I readjusted myself in my chair yet again as I shivered and I noticed my breath started to form long columns of vapour. I was running out of time before I had to make a jump to somewhere safe.

I flicked over the page on my holo-reader and I realised what had actually happened to this planet and I realised just how evil the Imperium was.

Back in the Keres-Human War, I had helped and studied and built the supernova Destroyer Class warships that had a weapon so powerful that a single blast could destroy an entire planet in a second.

Of course that warship was thankfully annihilated by the Keres towards the end of the war but the technology always remained. In fact, I had seen the technology used in everything from guns to missiles to laser weapons.

And an old boyfriend had told me that the supernova technology had recently been changed to superheat a planet and the Imperium was looking for testing sites.

Of course he wanted to know what planets I wanted dead, I said none, so I later found out that the Imperium had killed my ex-boyfriend for failing to find a planet. The Imperium was extremely weird like that.

A superheated blast would be more than possible to burn an entire world and if the Keres legends about Geneitor and Generatrix being able to sense life and death were true, then I have little doubt the God would have sent a warband there to make sure they collected the souls on his behalf.

I shivered at the very notion of what I had discovered and a small red flashing light appeared on my holo-console. I knew it was an Imperial Navy warship coming to kill me because that's the thing about the stupid Imperium.

You cannot say something against them. you cannot challenge them. And by the Rex, you certainly cannot discover the sheer power they hold because that means you know something they don't want you to know.

Meaning they cannot control you enough.

So I spun around on my black metal chair and with shaking hands I simply typed in coordinates to the Enlightened Republic, the little breakaway region of humanity that believed in peace, democracy and working with the Keres against the predations of the Imperium.

WAY OF THE ODYSSEY SHORT STORY COLLECTION
VOLUME 4

When I entered the Ultraspace network, a warning light told me three missiles were heading my way.

I zoomed off into the network and I was really looking forward to starting a brand-new life in the Republic, learning more about the Dark Keres and helping to protect humanity from both itself and the dark powers that stirred in the divine.

Lines were being drawn and sooner or later a massive fight between humanity, the different divisions of the Keres and the Republic would happen. And I just hoped for the sake of the innocent, that the right side won.

The ashes of Valican would always remind me why fighting against the Imperium and the Dark Keres were the most important things imaginable.

GET YOUR FREE SHORT STORY NOW!

And get signed up to Connor Whiteley's newsletter to hear about new gripping books, offers and exciting projects. (You'll never be sent spam)

https://www.subscribepage.io/garrosignup

WAY OF THE ODYSSEY SHORT STORY COLLECTION VOLUME 4

About the author:

Connor Whiteley is the author of over 60 books in the sci-fi fantasy, nonfiction psychology and books for writer's genre and he is a Human Branding Speaker and Consultant.

He is a passionate warhammer 40,000 reader, psychology student and author.

Who narrates his own audiobooks and he hosts The Psychology World Podcast.

All whilst studying Psychology at the University of Kent, England.

Also, he was a former Explorer Scout where he gave a speech to the Maltese President in August 2018 and he attended Prince Charles' 70th Birthday Party at Buckingham Palace in May 2018.

Plus, he is a self-confessed coffee lover!

Other books by Connor Whiteley:

Bettie English Private Eye Series
A Very Private Woman
The Russian Case
A Very Urgent Matter
A Case Most Personal
Trains, Scots and Private Eyes
The Federation Protects
Cops, Robbers and Private Eyes
Just Ask Bettie English
An Inheritance To Die For
The Death of Graham Adams
Bearing Witness
The Twelve
The Wrong Body
The Assassination Of Bettie English
Wining And Dying
Eight Hours
Uniformed Cabal
A Case Most Christmas

Gay Romance Novellas
Breaking, Nursing, Repairing A Broken Heart
Jacob And Daniel
Fallen For A Lie
Spying And Weddings
Clean Break

WAY OF THE ODYSSEY SHORT STORY COLLECTION VOLUME 4

Awakening Love
Meeting A Country Man
Loving Prime Minister
Snowed In Love
Never Been Kissed
Love Betrays You

<u>Lord of War Origin Trilogy:</u>
Not Scared Of The Dark
Madness
Burn Them All

<u>The Fireheart Fantasy Series</u>
Heart of Fire
Heart of Lies
Heart of Prophecy
Heart of Bones
Heart of Fate

<u>City of Assassins (Urban Fantasy)</u>
City of Death
City of Marytrs
City of Pleasure
City of Power

Agents of The Emperor
Return of The Ancient Ones
Vigilance
Angels of Fire
Kingmaker
The Eight
The Lost Generation
Hunt
Emperor's Council
Speaker of Treachery
Birth Of The Empire
Terraforma
Spaceguard

The Rising Augusta Fantasy Adventure Series
Rise To Power
Rising Walls
Rising Force
Rising Realm

Lord Of War Trilogy (Agents of The Emperor)
Not Scared Of The Dark
Madness
Burn It All Down

WAY OF THE ODYSSEY SHORT STORY COLLECTION VOLUME 4

Miscellaneous:
RETURN
FREEDOM
SALVATION
Reflection of Mount Flame
The Masked One
The Great Deer
English Independence

OTHER SHORT STORIES BY CONNOR WHITELEY

Mystery Short Story Collections
Criminally Good Stories Volume 1: 20 Detective Mystery Short Stories
Criminally Good Stories Volume 2: 20 Private Investigator Short Stories
Criminally Good Stories Volume 3: 20 Crime Fiction Short Stories
Criminally Good Stories Volume 4: 20 Science Fiction and Fantasy Mystery Short Stories
Criminally Good Stories Volume 5: 20 Romantic Suspense Short Stories

Mystery Short Stories:
Protecting The Woman She Hated
Finding A Royal Friend
Our Woman In Paris
Corrupt Driving
A Prime Assassination
Jubilee Thief
Jubilee, Terror, Celebrations
Negative Jubilation
Ghostly Jubilation
Killing For Womenkind
A Snowy Death
Miracle Of Death
A Spy In Rome
The 12:30 To St Pancreas
A Country In Trouble
A Smokey Way To Go
A Spicy Way To GO
A Marketing Way To Go
A Missing Way To Go
A Showering Way To Go
Poison In The Candy Cane
Kendra Detective Mystery Collection Volume 1
Kendra Detective Mystery Collection Volume 2
Mystery Short Story Collection Volume 1

WAY OF THE ODYSSEY SHORT STORY COLLECTION VOLUME 4

Mystery Short Story Collection Volume 2
Criminal Performance
Candy Detectives
Key To Birth In The Past

<u>Science Fiction Short Stories:</u>
Their Brave New World
Gummy Bear Detective
The Candy Detective
What Candies Fear
The Blurred Image
Shattered Legions
The First Rememberer
Life of A Rememberer
System of Wonder
Lifesaver
Remarkable Way She Died
The Interrogation of Annabella Stormic
Blade of The Emperor
Arbiter's Truth
Computation of Battle
Old One's Wrath
Puppets and Masters
Ship of Plague
Interrogation
Edge of Failure

Fantasy Short Stories:
City of Snow
City of Light
City of Vengeance
Dragons, Goats and Kingdom
Smog The Pathetic Dragon
Don't Go In The Shed
The Tomato Saver
The Remarkable Way She Died
Dragon Coins
Dragon Tea
Dragon Rider

All books in 'An Introductory Series':
Clinical Psychology and Transgender Clients
Clinical Psychology
Careers In Psychology
Psychology of Suicide
Dementia Psychology
Clinical Psychology Reflections Volume 4
Forensic Psychology of Terrorism And Hostage-Taking
Forensic Psychology of False Allegations
Year In Psychology
CBT For Anxiety
CBT For Depression
Applied Psychology

WAY OF THE ODYSSEY SHORT STORY COLLECTION VOLUME 4

BIOLOGICAL PSYCHOLOGY 3RD EDITION
COGNITIVE PSYCHOLOGY THIRD EDITION
SOCIAL PSYCHOLOGY- 3RD EDITION
ABNORMAL PSYCHOLOGY 3RD EDITION
PSYCHOLOGY OF RELATIONSHIPS- 3RD EDITION
DEVELOPMENTAL PSYCHOLOGY 3RD EDITION
HEALTH PSYCHOLOGY
RESEARCH IN PSYCHOLOGY
A GUIDE TO MENTAL HEALTH AND TREATMENT AROUND THE WORLD- A GLOBAL LOOK AT DEPRESSION
FORENSIC PSYCHOLOGY
THE FORENSIC PSYCHOLOGY OF THEFT, BURGLARY AND OTHER CRIMES AGAINST PROPERTY
CRIMINAL PROFILING: A FORENSIC PSYCHOLOGY GUIDE TO FBI PROFILING AND GEOGRAPHICAL AND STATISTICAL PROFILING.
CLINICAL PSYCHOLOGY
FORMULATION IN PSYCHOTHERAPY
PERSONALITY PSYCHOLOGY AND

INDIVIDUAL DIFFERENCES
CLINICAL PSYCHOLOGY REFLECTIONS VOLUME 1
CLINICAL PSYCHOLOGY REFLECTIONS VOLUME 2
Clinical Psychology Reflections Volume 3
CULT PSYCHOLOGY
Police Psychology

A Psychology Student's Guide To University
How Does University Work?
A Student's Guide To University And Learning
University Mental Health and Mindset

www.ingramcontent.com/pod-product-compliance
Lightning Source LLC
LaVergne TN
LVHW012126070526
838202LV00056B/5881